© London Regional Transport 1996

INTRODUCTION

Before you read the *Underneath the Underground* stories, it is important you understand what the London Underground system is all about. As you will know, London is the capital city of England and home to many famous names and places. There are museums, shops, theatres and restaurants. You can walk, take a taxi, or catch a bus to all these things, but what a lot of people in London do is board a train. Now these are not ordinary trains . . . they are known as tube trains and they run on a railway network called the London Underground, hidden well away, far below the bustling city streets. Take a look at the Underground map and you will see all the different rail lines, colour coded, and lots of station stops dotted along them. If, one day, you happen to be at any one of these stations, waiting on the platform for a train, you may look down and see a small mouse or two scurrying along the rail track. They might be playing, gathering food, perhaps visiting friends or relatives . . . but as soon as they hear that distant rumble, and then that loud roar as a train speeds into the station, they will quickly and quietly disappear from sight.

So where are they running to? Well, these brave and hardy London mice are heading for the safety of their own world . . . Underneath the Underground.

ANTHEA TURNER & WENDY TURNER

UNDERNEATH the UNDERGROUND

The Ghost of Knightsbridge

PUFFIN BOOKS

THE GHOST OF KNIGHTSBRIDGE

Nigel Knight stood on the pavement at the entrance of Knightsbridge Tube Station and breathed in the cold night air. It was ten minutes to midnight on 26th October and Nigel had just felt the first bitter chill of winter. And Nigel should know. He left his underground home every night at ten to twelve and sat on the pavement outside the tube station. Spring, summer, autumn or winter, Nigel never missed an opportunity to feast his eyes upon the shop called Harrods. The building was covered with white fairy lights and every night they sparkled like diamonds against the jet-black sky. Nigel sat and gazed.

It was special . . . magical . . . it was Harrods, the most spectacular, most famous department store in the whole world! The fairy lights would be turned off soon. It was nearly midnight and any minute now the beautiful red brick building would be lost against the dark winter sky.

Nigel shivered and pushed his two front paws even deeper into the pockets of his thick woollen coat. He must be getting back to his home soon, deep underground. His family were making big plans for a Halloween party to be held this coming Monday, 31st October, and he really should be helping out. What fun it was going to be. All those ghosts and ghouls, spooks and spirits. Of course Nigel didn't really believe in Halloween ghosts, but nevertheless it was all very exciting.

In fact, when Nigel came to think about it, there was always an air of excitement at Knightsbridge Tube Station. The place just never stopped buzzing, what with all the London tourists chattering about the many amazing shops they had been to, especially Harrods. The mice had heard many wonderful stories about the enormous department store. Everyone said the Food Halls were a sight to behold and there were so many different cheeses on display it was simply impossible to keep a count of them all.

'One day,' Nigel promised himself, 'one day I'm going to find a way into Harrods and see the great cheese counter for myself!'

Brave words indeed, for it was not going to be easy. The Security Cats there had fierce reputations, and if Nigel was going to explore the Food Halls he wanted to live to tell the tale.

The lights that decorated the outside of Harrods went out and at that precise moment Nigel realised his chance to see the cheese counter was just around the corner. The night of Halloween presented the perfect opportunity for such an adventure and he had thought of a plan that couldn't possibly fail.

Meanwhile, underneath the Underground at Knightsbridge Tube Station, the rest of the Knight family were busy making preparations for the forthcoming Halloween party, to be held at their home on 31st October. Nigel's mum and dad, Doris and Vincent, had three little mice in their family. There was Nigel, who was the eldest, and then the twins, Neil and Nancy. Their home could be reached by way of a small hole at the side of one of the rail tracks on Platform 2. A short tunnel led further underground and eventually on to the spacious home of the Knight family. There was much activity there on this particular evening. It was very late, but there was a big party to organise and some mice found themselves working around the clock to make sure it was a great success.

Little Neil and Nancy were in the living room making paper lanterns. They had been collecting old tube train tickets for the best part of a week and were now using them to make Chinese lanterns of all sizes.

'We must make plenty in time for the party!' declared Neil.

Nancy agreed and set to work even faster than before.

'Neil,' she said, drawing a deep breath before she asked the question, 'Do you believe in ghosts?'

Neil stopped what he was doing and frowned.

'Well,' he said, 'I don't think I've ever seen a real ghost, or a witch or a ghoul or anything like that. I tell you what though, I think this Halloween party of ours is going to be very spooky.'

'Yes,' replied Nancy. 'That's what I'm afraid of.'

The two small mice fell silent and with nimble paws began work again on their very beautiful Chinese lanterns.

Vincent was sitting in the kitchen with a Salesmouse from the Underground newspaper, the *Daily Tail*. Although he had already sent out some personal invitations, Vincent wanted to advertise the Halloween party to all the mice who lived on the London Underground, and now he and the

Salesmouse were going over the details of the advertisement.

'How about this for the final line,' said the Salesmouse. **'Only the very bravest of mice need attend**!'

'Brilliant!' shouted Vincent, banging his paw down on the kitchen table. He chuckled to himself as the Salesmouse made notes. Old Tosh Archer from Marble Arch Tube Station has some wonderful ghost stories to tell. You'd have to be a brave mouse indeed to hear some of those to the end.

Doris heard the raised voices in the kitchen and smiled to herself. She was standing in the hall watching two large black spiders measure up the doorways for some custom-made cobwebs. The giant furry creatures were a rather jolly husband and wife team who lived at Hyde Park Corner, just one station stop eastbound on the Piccadilly Line.

'We've been asked to make cobwebs before,' announced one of the spiders, 'but we've never tackled a job as big as this.'

Doris looked worried and the spider guessed what she was thinking.

'Now don't you worry about a thing, Mrs Knight. We'll spin all the cobwebs in good time for your party and the quality of the threads will be second to none.'

At the stroke of midnight the Salesmouse and the two spiders departed and just two minutes later Nigel appeared at the front door, glad to be back in the warmth of his family home.

'And how did Harrods look tonight?' His mum asked him.

'Oh, as grand as ever,' replied Nigel.

'And are you looking forward to the party?' his mum continued.

'Oh yes,' he said. 'I can't wait for Halloween to arrive!'

Nigel's mind was racing with thoughts and plans for the night of 31st October. He would be at the party, that was for sure, but not all night, oh no. He had a plan that would get him past the Security Cat and into Harrods. He was going to spend Halloween exploring the Food Halls of the most famous department store in the world!

That night each member of the Knight family dreamt of Halloween, each little mouse praying hard that any talk of spooks and spirits in Knightsbridge was only make-believe.

Two days later, acceptance letters for the party began pouring in. Every mouse on the Underground had seen the invitation printed in the *Daily Tail*, and the very bravest of them had no intention of missing the Halloween party. Now, the question every mouse had to consider was, what to wear? Fancy-dress costumes were an absolute must and if they were to be any good at all there was simply no time to lose in making them.

'Ouch!' yelled Nigel as he bumped into an arm of the settee, squashing his nose against the cushions. He scrabbled about under the large white handkerchief that was covering him, eventually managing to pull it off and throw it on to the floor.

'Honestly!' he exclaimed. 'There's more to being a ghost than meets the eye!'

Neil and Nancy giggled loudly at their older brother until he too saw the funny side and roared with laughter.

'I'll just have to make these eyeholes a little larger,' he informed the twins, and set to work with Doris's sewing scissors. His costume had to be perfect. After all, he could hardly get past the Harrods Security Cat if he couldn't see where he was going.

Not too far away, on a different part of the Knightsbridge Underground, a group of Harrods Security Cats were taking a well-earned afternoon tea break. The Security Cats had a very important job. They were employed by the famous store to guard a network of private tunnels running between Harrods and its enormous warehouse in nearby Trevor Square. Special green and gold Harrods trucks ran to and fro all the time, and it was the job of the Security Cats to stop any naughty mice or other adventurous creatures running through the tunnels and into the Harrods store. A large ginger cat put down his mug of milk and gave out a large yawn.

'Well, that's my shift over. Not on now until Monday night.'

A much smaller black cat almost choked on his sardine sandwich.

'Monday night? Oh my eyebrows and whiskers!'

'Pull yourself together, lad,' snapped the ginger cat. He was head of the Security Department and liked to assert his authority whenever possible. 'What on earth is the matter?'

The black cat's throat had gone quite dry and it was a good few seconds before he could manage a reply.

14

'Have you forgotten what date it is, boss? When you do your shift tomorrow night, it'll be . . . HALLOWEEN!'

There was a deadly silence as all the cats in the group took in this rather worrying piece of information. The ginger cat was the first to speak.

'Oh for goodness sake,' he said, his voice shaking only very slightly. 'Who ever believes in ghosts? Let me tell you, I've been working here now for five long years and I've never seen a witch or a ghost or anything even a little bit spooky.'

'Aha,' said a sharp-witted tabby cat, 'but the question is, have you ever been down here on the night of Halloween before?'

The ginger cat froze as all eyes gazed upon him waiting for the reply. In five years he had never had to work on 31st October.

'No,' he answered, trying to sound as brave as possible. 'Now you come to mention it, I don't believe that I have . . .'

When Nigel Knight woke on Monday 31st October, the first thing he did was breathe in the unmistakeable smell of treacle toffee. It was a fantastic smell and so strong Nigel wouldn't have been surprised if the mice who lived at Piccadilly Circus could smell it too. He knew at once, of course, where the smell was coming from. His mum was already busy making toffee apples and preparing great dishes full of pumpkin pie for the Halloween party. Nigel crept into the twins' room and gave them both a shake and a prod. In a second they were shrieking and tugging at his ears and whiskers, convinced that a Halloween spook had woken them from their dreams.

'My oh my,' thought Nigel when Neil and Nancy had at last calmed down. 'Party fever has started early.' Then he

16

remembered the wonderful adventure he had planned for that night and he too felt a strange shiver of excitement creeping down his spine.

'Come on you lot,' shouted Vincent. 'Let's get these lanterns hung up before the custom-made cobwebs arrive.'

'We're coming, dad!' the three mice shouted back and scurried into the living room as fast as they could.

For five hours they all worked, baking party food and decorating the house with Chinese lanterns, witches' broomsticks and paper skeletons, and by the time the spiders had finished spinning their cobwebs around the doorways the stage was set for the party of a lifetime.

'Right,' said Doris, taking command, 'I want everyone to have a good wash and brush-up and get changed into their party costumes. We've got plenty of time before the guests start arriving at six.'

The rest of the Knight family obediently set about tidying themselves up, brushing their fur and cleaning their ears before putting on their Halloween party costumes. Vincent thought he looked very dashing as Count Dracula. The black silk neck scarf he had found a few weeks earlier made an excellent cape.

People were so careless with things like scarves and handkerchiefs. It was a good job the Underground mice were able to make good use of them. Doris was dressed up as a witch in a slinky black dress and pointed hat and the twins were dressed in green as a pair of hobgoblins.

Nigel threw the white handkerchief over himself and arranged it so he could see out of the two holes he had cut for the eyes. He peered into the mirror and chuckled at the thing staring back at him. It was a ghost, the very ghost that was going to get him past the Security Cat and into Harrods.

'Are you ready, Nigel?' shouted Doris. 'We're all here in the kitchen.'

'Coming, mum!' Nigel yelled back and made his way to the kitchen where his mum, dad, brother and sister were parading up and down admiring each other's costumes. Nigel burst in through the kitchen door, flapping his paws about and making  ghost-like noises. The other mice screamed and giggled and looked suitably impressed, making Nigel believe more than ever that his ghostly outfit was going to give the Harrods Security Cat the fright of his life.

'Let's go into the living room and wait for our guests in there,' suggested Vincent, but no sooner had he said it than

a loud knock came at the door. RAT A TAT TAT. The Knight family could hardly contain themselves. It was old Tosh Archer from Marble Arch Tube Station, followed closely by the rest of the Archer family. The party had begun. In fact they barely had time to exchange 'hellos' and marvel at each other's

outfits before another loud knock came at the door, followed by another and another. Mice from all over the London Underground scampered into Knightsbridge, every single one of them trying not to show how relieved they were at being in the safe and secure surroundings of the Knights' lovely home.

Some of the mice had travelled a great distance on the Underground network to get to Knightsbridge, balancing for ages on the footplates in between the train carriages. It had been a long and tiring journey for many of them, not helped by meeting other party-goers along the way. There had been several frightening moments as mice dressed up as

EASTBOUND TRAINS

HIGH ST. KENSINGTON
PADDINGTON

FOR
VICTORIA
EMBANKMENT

BOW ROAD
SQUEAKING

Halloween spooks bumped into each other down in the dark tube tunnels, and by the time they reached Knightsbridge, all their nerves were on edge.

At about six-thirty Tosh Archer did a quick head count and reported to Doris and Vincent that just about all those who were expected to attend had indeed arrived. He stood on a chair in the hall and shouted at the top of his voice.

'Listen, everyone! The first ghost story, as told by me, will start in exactly two minutes. All those who want to hear this chilling tale, please assemble in the living room and take your seats by the fire. And don't forget, folks, as the invitation said, "**only the very bravest of mice need attend**"!'

A group of church mice from St Paul's decided that they were suddenly very hungry and made their way to the kitchen. Martha Bell from Belsize Park Tube Station said she simply must have a nap before she could enjoy the party properly, and Connie Conqueror from Tower Hill muttered  something about powdering her nose. Tosh Archer's announcement had split the mice into two very separate camps: the brave and not-so-brave. For the next half hour the not-so-brave would avoid the living room at all costs, while the brave were already fighting for the best seats.

'Settle down now, settle down,' said Tosh, and took a long hard look at all the mice surrounding him. A sea of faces

stared back, desperate for the ghost story to begin. Some of the younger mice were fidgeting terribly, tugging at their whiskers and pulling each other's tails. Tosh gave an extra long stare at these little mice until eventually everyone was silent and very, very still.

'Anyone for pumpkin pie?' Doris shouted, poking her head around the door.

Without exception each mouse leapt from his seat. The creaking of the door and Doris's loud voice had given them a great shock, just when the ghost story was about to begin!

'Good gracious, Doris,' Vincent grumbled, settling himself down again. 'What a moment to choose!'

Tosh Archer demanded silence once more and without further delay began his tale.

Doris crept out and made her way back to the kitchen. She opened the oven door and put back the pumpkin pie. Connie Conqueror came into the kitchen with a freshly powdered nose. She was glad to find Doris there. The two mice hadn't met for some time and there was a lot of news to catch up on. Connie enjoyed telling Doris of her recent adventure. She was of royal descent, and she had worn her diamond tiara at a summer garden party. A magpie had seen it sparkling in the sunlight and taken a fancy to it. Quick as a flash he had swooped down and taken it in his beak. It had taken a lot of effort to get it back and

Connie took great delight in telling the story to anyone who would listen.

Meanwhile, in the living room, Tosh was coming to the end of his story . . .

'Young Billy Bayswater heard the clock strike ten as he leapt off the platform on to the tube train. There was an old man sitting in the carriage, no one else, and Billy tucked himself away by the gentleman's feet. The train pulled out of the station and as if from nowhere another mouse appeared, dressed from top to tail in a ticket collector's uniform, with the beck of his cap pulled right down over his face.

"Ticket please, sonny," he said to Bill, and it was at this point in time that Billy knew something was wrong. "Ticket?" he said. "I don't need a ticket. This is a train for humans and I'm just along for the ride. Bond Street to Green Park and back again!" The ticket collector mouse shook his head very slowly.

"Sorry, sonny, but this isn't a return journey. You'll not be getting off here again. We're on a one-way trip . . . to the end of the line."

The ticket collector mouse took hold of his cap and pushed it up behind his ears. Billy Bayswater stared. He tried to move but his legs were as heavy as lead. You see, the ticket collector mouse hadn't got dark fur like you and me. He was PURE WHITE, and Billy realised . . . that the train he was on . . . was a GHOST train!'

Tosh sat back and listened to the gasp of amazement from his audience.

'A GHOST train,' they repeated. 'So that's what those other mice were trying to warn Billy of!'

'That's right,' said Tosh triumphantly. 'But I want you all to remember it's just a story I've heard and there might not be any truth in it at all. White mice probably don't exist . . . well, I've never seen one. So don't you all go dreaming about ghost trains tonight. Now, let's have some music. I want to *see* everyone dancing!'

Nigel crept quietly out of the room as the music blared from the record player. The party was in full swing and no one would miss him for the next hour or so. He stopped by the hall mirror and made sure that his ghost costume was on properly. It was time for a sightseeing trip to Harrods, and with the great cheese counter foremost in his mind, he opened the front door and headed off into the cold, dark night.

In about ten minutes he arrived at the private network of tunnels that belonged to the famous department store and immediately wondered if the whole thing was such a good idea after all. It was deadly quiet and the green and gold Harrods trucks that ran along the tracks were sitting quietly in the shadows. Nigel shivered. Thoughts of cheese counters had given way to thoughts of ghost trains and he ran past the small trucks as fast as his legs would carry him.

A little further up the tunnel the large ginger cat was pacing up and down.

'Got to keep moving,' he was thinking to himself. 'Got to keep busy.'

He didn't like this Halloween business. He didn't like it

one little bit. He shone his torch down one of the tunnels. Surely that was a rustling he could hear. The torchlight didn't reveal anything, however, and he began pacing up and down once more.

After a minute he stopped. He could hear something and if his ears were to be trusted that something was almost right behind him. He swung around and, as Nigel had planned, got the fright of his life. The ginger cat sprang into the air and all the fur on his body stood on end. It was a ghost, a real live ghost, and he was not going to stick around to say 'hello'.

With much hissing and meowing, he bolted for home. Nigel watched him go and without further delay made his way to the entrance the ginger cat was supposed to be guarding. All the doors were wide open and Nigel resolved to close them on his way out in case the poor cat got into trouble with the owners of the store. The tunnel Nigel had come

through was called Wine Cellar Close. This led directly into the wine cellar, which in turn led into the Harrods Food Halls. He pulled off his ghost costume and stood for a moment, taking in the full glory of the famous store. It was simply enormous, but most of all it was very, very beautiful.

The floors were made of marble and the walls were covered in shiny tiles. Nigel sniffed the air. He ran in one direction and stopped. He sniffed the air again. Nothing. He ran in the opposite direction and smelt . . . cheese! He ran into the next Food Hall and there, opposite the cake counter, stood row upon row of cheeses. There was every kind of cheese you could possibly think of: hard cheese, soft cheese, goats' cheese, English cheese, French cheese . . . it went on and on and on. There was just one small problem. All the cheeses were covered up. It was very disappointing. He had come all this way and a large, thick piece of glass stood between him and the most wonderful feast any mouse could imagine.

He sighed heavily and turned his back on the Harrods cheese counter. The adventure wasn't over yet. There was something else in Harrods he wanted to see and that was the Toy Kingdom. He rushed over to read the store guide but was met with another disappointment. The Toy Kingdom was on the fourth floor. He sulked for a moment or two before scampering off to see what else he could find on the ground floor. He was just running past the lifts when he heard voices coming towards him. They were human voices and he darted behind a potted plant as the footsteps got closer.

'See you tomorrow night then, Jack. I'll just finish up round here then I'll be on my way.'

Nigel poked his head around the plant pot. It was a cleaning lady talking to a security guard.

'Right you are then, Doreen,' replied the security guard. He reached out and pushed a button that made the lift doors slide open. 'I'm just off to check out some of the other floors . . . goodnight.'

Nigel spotted his chance and took it. In a few leaps and bounds he was in the lift and snuggled into the corner, and that's where he stayed until eventually the security guard stopped the lift at the fourth floor.

Nigel arrived at the Toy Kingdom and let out a long whistle. There were toys and games of every description. He looked at the soft toys. There were small bears and dolls right through to giant pandas and giraffes. A notice stood at the side of this dazzling array:

TOY KINGDOM
Customers are kindly requested
not to touch or feed the animals
Thank you
Harrods

Nigel had no intention whatsoever of touching the animals. They looked a pretty quiet lot but they were all much bigger than he was, and he didn't fancy getting on the wrong side of the huge hippopotamus that was standing in the corner. He crept through an archway to the electronic games section and climbed into a four-wheel-drive truck. He touched the pedal with one of his back paws and gripped on to the steering wheel as the truck shot forward. This was fun! He went round and round in circles before pointing the truck in a straight line and guiding it out of the Toy Kingdom and towards the main stairway. Why bother waiting for the lift? Tackling the stairs with this truck was going to be much more exciting!

The large black rubber wheels bounced down the stairs, slowly at first and then faster and faster . . . Nigel realised the large truck was quite out of control! It bounced, lurched and skidded until at last the truck and Nigel bumped into a wall and came to a complete halt. He was a little dazed but it didn't take him long to recover.

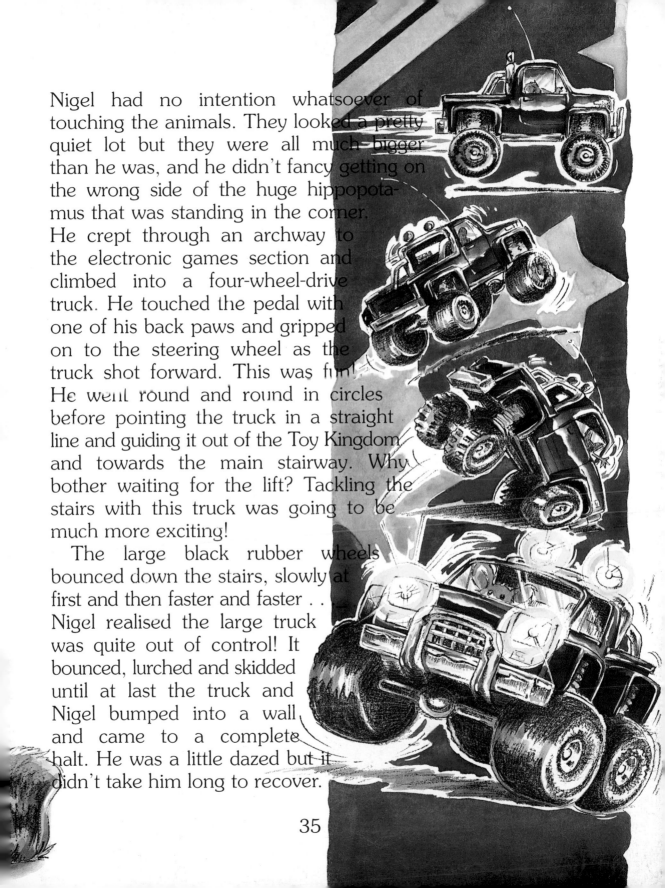

35

He drove over to the store guide and discovered he was on floor number two, home of the pet department. Nigel thought how marvellous it would be to say 'hello' to the animals, and without hesitation he drove the truck forward and followed the arrows to the pets. Faster and faster went the truck, through the luggage department and on through the dress materials until Nigel came to the entrance to the pet department and stamped his paw hard on the brake. He climbed out of the truck and started to inspect the rows of cages. It was very quiet. There were rabbits and guinea pigs and exotic birds but they all had their eyes shut and in one corner there was a rabbit snoring quite loudly. Nigel stuck his nose through the bars of a small silver cage but couldn't see anything. He thought the cage was empty but noticed some movement in a ball of straw at the back.

'Hey!' he whispered. 'Anybody at home?'

The ball of straw moved again and out from the middle of it came a mouse . . . a pure . . . white . . . mouse! Nigel tried to move but, like little Billy Bayswater in Tosh Archer's ghost story, his legs felt as heavy as lead. He stared at the white mouse and the white mouse stared back. Nigel Knight had never been so frightened in his whole life. Surely the whole thing was some terrible nightmare. Surely in just a moment he would wake up, snug and warm and safe in his own bed.

The white mouse in the cage took a couple of steps forward and waved to Nigel.

'Hello!' he said.

A talking ghost was too much for Nigel and he let out the most almighty scream. 'Aaaarrgghhh!' It lasted a good few seconds and woke up every pet in the pet department.

'Oh my goodness me,' complained a grey rabbit. 'What is all the fuss about?'

'Yes,' continued a brightly coloured parrot, sounding very grumpy indeed. 'Come over here, brown mouse, and explain yourself . . . How on earth did you get in?'

The other animals gave Nigel some confidence but he still couldn't take his eyes off the white mouse. It must be the most life-like ghost anyone had ever seen!

'The white mmmmouse,' stuttered Nigel. 'Tonight is the night of Halloween and that white mouse is a ghost!'

'I can assure you that I am not!' snapped the white mouse. 'Come over here and shake my paw. You'll soon see that I'm flesh and blood. Still, on second thoughts perhaps you had better not shake my paw. Where on earth have you been to get your white fur so dirty?'

'Dirty?' shouted Nigel. 'Dirty? I'll have you know that I wash twice a day and my daddy says I'm about the cleanest mouse on the Underground!'

At that, everyone started talking at once. What was it like to live Underneath the Underground? Had all the mice there got dark fur? How had Nigel got into Harrods and what, exactly, was Halloween? For the next 20 minutes Nigel and the pets swapped stories and Nigel was at last convinced that the white mouse was not a Halloween ghost.

All the pets were fascinated, not to mention a tiny bit envious of Nigel's life on the London Underground, but none so much as the white mouse. He told his story to Nigel. Up until Saturday there had been seven white mice in his cage, but a customer had come into the department and wanted to buy only six. With his companions gone, the white mouse who was left was longing for some company and excitement, and could think of nothing better than going home with Nigel and living on the London Underground.

'Take me with you,' he pleaded, but Nigel wasn't so sure. The white mouse was very friendly and Nigel would love to take him to meet all his friends. But was it fair? Life on the Underground was very different to life in the Harrods Pet Department.

In the end they had a vote. They discussed the matter back and forth and then everyone voiced their opinion. What they decided was this: the white mouse would go home tonight with Nigel and over the next week Nigel would take him on a grand tour of the Underground. If he liked it that was fine and he would set up home and stay. If he thought he wasn't going to be happy there, Nigel would think of a foolproof plan to get the mouse back into Harrods and into the pet department. Then there was the question of a name. The white mouse had no name until everyone agreed that surely 'Harry' was the most appropriate name a Harrods mouse could have. So Harry it was, and in no time at all Nigel had opened the cage and was showing Harry the four-wheel-drive truck that would get them out of the store. Nigel sat behind the wheel and Harry climbed in beside him.

'Goodbye Harry! Good luck!'

Harry turned and waved to all the pets, and they waved back and shouted goodbye. He was quite sad to be leaving. A tear started forming in the corner of his eye but he thought of the wonderful life he was going to have on the London Underground and brushed the tear away quickly. Nigel put his foot

down hard on the pedal and they were off; back through the dress materials and luggage and through to the main stairs. Nigel pointed the truck towards the stairs and told Harry to hold on tight. Down the stairs they bounced, faster and faster, screeching around the corners to get the truck on to the next set of stairs that would take them down another floor. Just when Harry thought he could take no more, a most welcome sign came into view. 'Ground Floor' it read and at long last the bumpy ride was over.

The mice abandoned the truck behind one of the cosmetic counters and scampered back through the Food Halls, eventually arriving at the doorway Nigel had come through a good two hours before. Harry wanted to linger at the cheese counter but Nigel urged him to keep going. The Halloween party back home would be ending soon and if Nigel was missed it would cause a lot of upset and ruin the night.

So on they both scampered, through the wine cellar and into the private underground tunnels. Harry had never known such excitement. He was quite out of breath and had to hold on to Nigel's tail so as not to get lost in the dark nooks and crannies.

'Here we are, Harry,' said Nigel. 'Our front door is just around the corner!'

The two mice could hear music, shouting and laughter. Obviously the party was still in full swing. They opened the front door and crept into the hall. It sounded as if everyone was in the living room. Nigel burst through the door, waving his paws in the air.

'Hello, everyone! Meet my friend Harry!'

Nigel and Harry stood grinning by the door while panic broke out all around them. Tosh Archer sat down and rubbed his eyes in disbelief. Some young mice screamed in terror and ran out of the room. Vincent and Doris Knight felt all their fur stand on end. Martha Bell fainted and the group of church mice from St Paul's began to pray.

'Of course,' thought Nigel, who had by now got quite used to the idea of Harry being white, 'they all think they've seen a ghost!'

He saw the look of utter shock on the faces surrounding him and began to explain very quickly what had happened. Great gasps of amazement could be heard around the room as Nigel revealed that Harry was not a Halloween ghost, but a pure white mouse from Harrods. Martha Bell began to recover and the church mice thanked the Lord that Harry was not the ghost of little Billy Bayswater coming back to haunt them. Vincent and Doris began introducing Harry to all the party guests and once they had heard the full story, insisted that Harry stay with them as long as he liked. Nigel got a bit of a telling-off for planning such a dangerous adventure, but his mum and dad didn't stay cross with him for long. For a mouse to be so close to some of the greatest cheeses in the world and not be able to sample any of them was punishment enough.

Harry chattered away happily to his new friends and thought how marvellous it was going to be living with the Knight family on the London Underground. He knew for sure there would be no question of him wanting to go back to his old life in the pet department. Doris made pumpkin soup and toast as a late-night supper, and it was just when everyone was tucking into second helpings that the clock on the wall struck midnight. All the mice breathed a sigh of relief. Halloween was well and truly over!

On Tuesday 1st November, while all the Underground mice were having a lie-in due to the party the night before, Jack, the Harrods security guard, was having a tea break at the end of his night shift.

'I just can't understand it,' he said to his friend Colin, who was about to go on duty. 'How does a truck get from the

Toy Kingdom down to the cosmetics department? And look at this . . . a white handkerchief with two small holes cut in it was found in the Food Hall. It's puzzling me, I can tell you.'

Colin shook his head. 'Can't say I know how either of them could have got there . . . You didn't hear anything last night then? Fairly quiet, was it?'

'Quiet? Oh yes,' replied Jack, 'Quiet as a mouse . . .'

© London Regional Transport 1996

Underneath the Underground is dedicated to The Humane Research Trust, a registered charity which raises funds to develop alternative methods to the use of animals in medical research. For further information please write to The Humane Research Trust, 29 Bramhall Lane South, Bramhall, Cheshire, SK7 2DN or telephone 0161–439 8041.

PUFFIN BOOKS

Published by the Penguin Group
Penguin Books Ltd, 27 Wrights Lane, London W8 5TZ, England
Penguin Putnam Inc., 375 Hudson Street, New York, New York 10014, USA
Penguin Books Australia Ltd, Ringwood, Victoria, Australia
Penguin Books Canada Ltd, 10 Alcorn Avenue, Toronto, Ontario, Canada M4V 3B2
Penguin Books (NZ) Ltd, 182–190 Wairau Road, Auckland 10, New Zealand

Penguin Books Ltd, Registered Offices: Harmondsworth, Middlesex, England

First published by The Book Guild Ltd 1996
Published in Puffin Books 1998
1 3 5 7 9 10 8 6 4 2

Made and printed in Italy by Printers srl – Trento

British Library Cataloguing in Publication Data
A CIP catalogue record for this book is available from the British Library

ISBN 0–140–56388–1